About Me

This is a drawing of me.

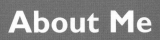

My name is ....

I am .... years old.

I especially like to draw ....
....

My favorite color is ....

I like collecting ....
....

My Family

This is a drawing of my family.

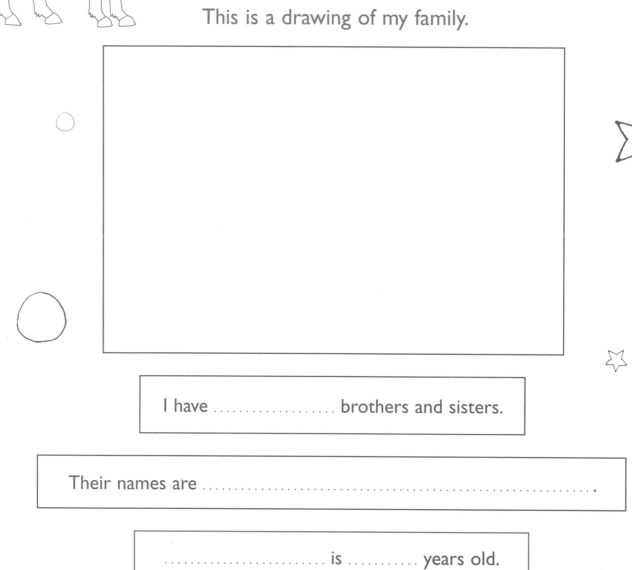

I have .... brothers and sisters.

Their names are ....

.... is .... years old.

.... is .... years old.

They like to play ....

We like to .... when we are together.

My Friends

This is a drawing of my friends.

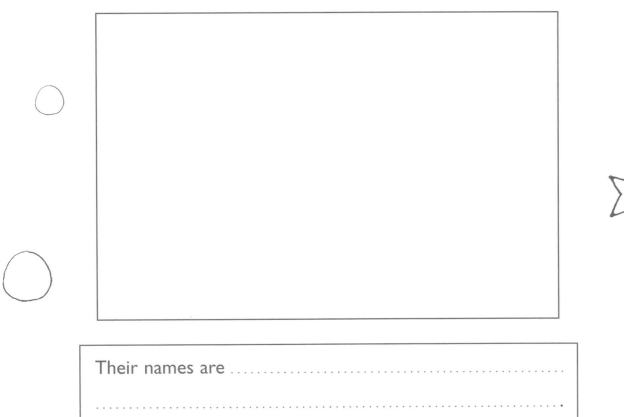

Their names are ....
....

We like to play ....
....

I am taller than ....

I can run faster than ....

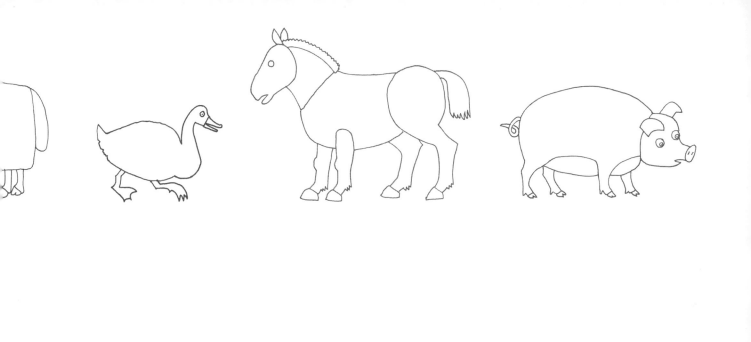

My Room

This is a drawing of my room.

My favorite toy in my room is ....

My bed is the color ....

This is what my room looks like before I put away all of my toys.

My Pet

This is a drawing of my pet.

His name is . . . .

He is a . . . .

We like to play . . . .

His favorite toy is . . . .

He likes to eat . . . . for dinner.

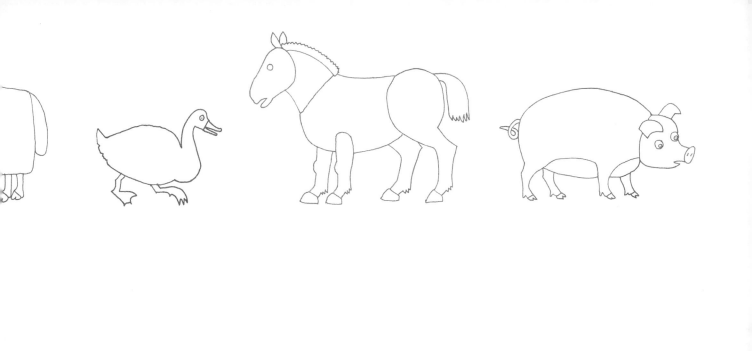

the world of
ERiC CARLE®

ISBN 978-0-448-45085-8   10 9 8 7 6 5 4 3 2 1

To find out more about Eric Carle books, visit www.eric-carle.com
To find out about The Eric Carle Museum of Picture Book Art,
visit www.picturebookart.org